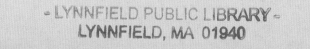

Printed in Malaysia
First Edition
1 3 5 7 9 10 8 6 4 2
H106-9333-5-14305

Text is set in Rockwell Regular
Art is created using iDraw and SketchBook Pro on an iPad

Designed by Tyler Nevins
Reinforced binding

Library of Congress Cataloging-in-Publication Data

Gude, Paul, author, illustrator.
 A surprise for Giraffe and Elephant / Paul Gude.—First edition.
     pages cm
 Summary: Quiet Giraffe and chatty Elephant have a friendship that sees them
through misunderstanding, disappointment, and an interesting surprise.
  ISBN 978-1-4231-8311-2 (alk. paper)
 [1. Friendship—Fiction. 2. Elephants—Fiction. 3. Giraffe—Fiction.] I. Title.
 PZ7.G93482Sur 2015
 [E]—dc23   2013041062

Visit www.DisneyBooks.com

a surprise for Giraffe and ELEPHANT

by Paul Gude

Disney • Hyperion Books
New York

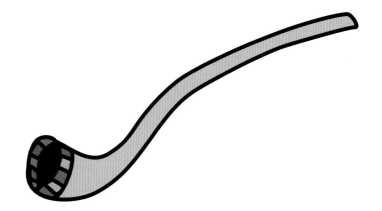

THE BEST TIME

Elephant was woken up by a very loud noise.

It was Giraffe, playing his alpine horn.

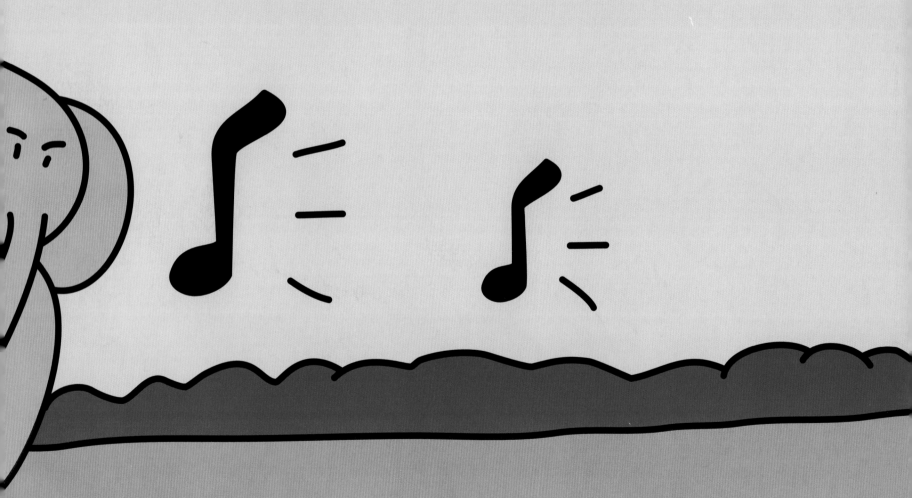

"Giraffe!" said Elephant. "It's too early for alpine horns!"

That night, when Elephant was sleeping,
Giraffe started playing again.

"Giraffe!" said Elephant. "It's too late for alpine horns!"

The next day, Elephant found
Giraffe's alpine horn in the trash.

"Poor Giraffe," said Elephant.

"How will you ever know the best time for alpine horns if you never ask?"

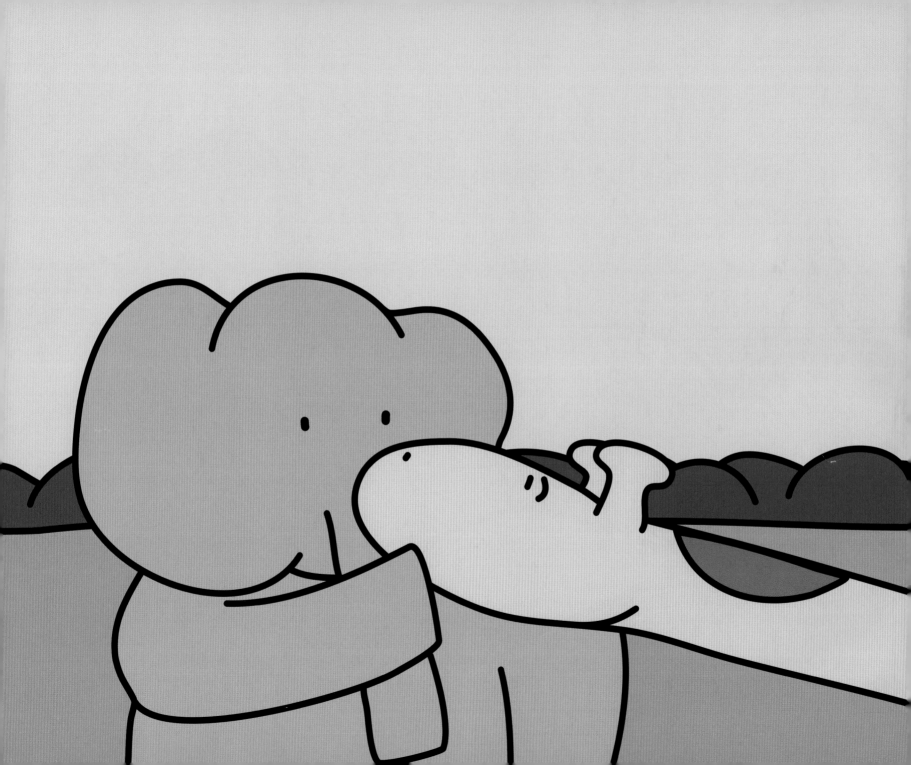

At lunch, Giraffe wanted to play while Elephant ate her sandwich.

It was the best time for alpine horns.

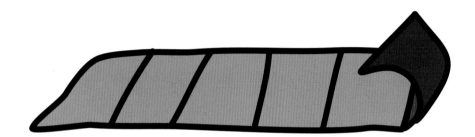

The Toboggan

"I want a toboggan!" said Elephant.

"It's like a sled," she explained. "It goes very fast."

Giraffe decided to build a toboggan.

He worked all night.

Elephant couldn't wait to try it.

It wasn't as much fun as she thought it would be.

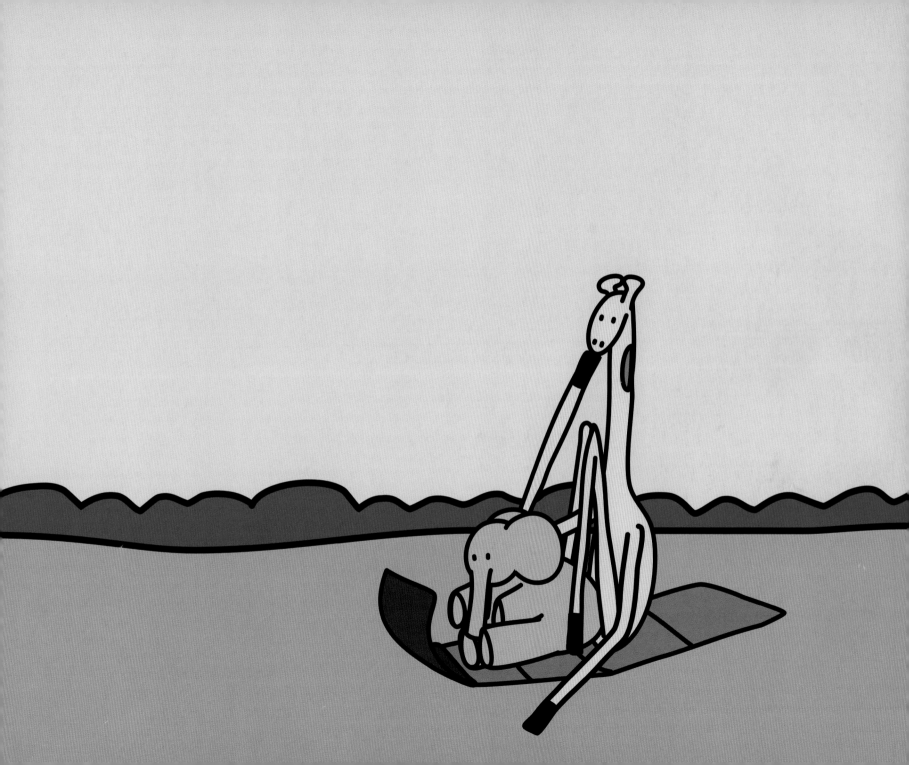

"You know what would be REALLY fun?" asked Elephant.
"A bobsled!"

Giraffe didn't say anything.

GIRAFFE'S SURPRISE PARTY

"I'm going to throw you a surprise party," said Elephant.
"Make a list of what you want."

Since Giraffe could not explain what "surprise" meant, he kept his list simple.

Elephant worked all day.

"Okay!" yelled "Elephant. "It's time for your surprise!"

All of their animal friends
were covered with balloons.

Giraffe's boom box was covered with polka dots.

"I really know how to make a surprise party!"
said Elephant.

Giraffe agreed. Completely.

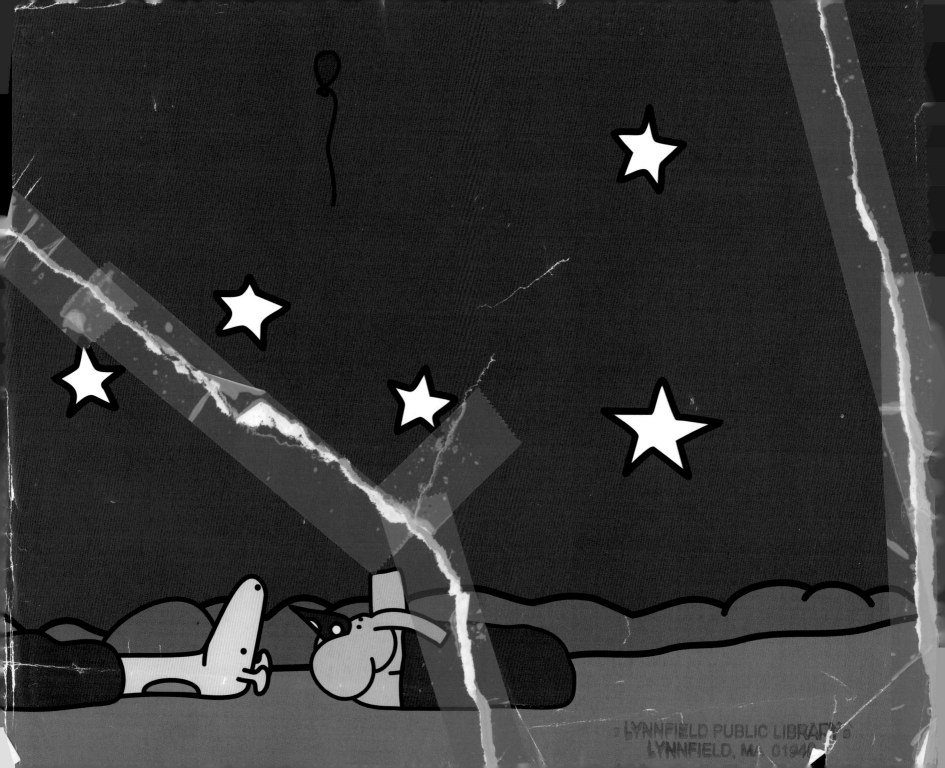